Among the Untamed

Among the Untamed

dee Hobsbawn-Smith

Frontenac House Poetry

Copyright © 2023 dee Hobsbawn-Smith
All rights reserved, including moral rights. No part of this publication may be reproduced or transmitted in any form or by any means, electronic or mechanical, including photocopying, recording, or from any information storage retrieval system, without permission in writing from the author, publisher, or ACCESS copyright, except by a reviewer or academic who may quote brief passages in a review or critical study.

Book design: Neil Petrunia
Cover Image: *The Reckoner* – Stacey Walyuchow
Author photo: Richard Marjan

Library and Archives Canada Cataloguing in Publication

Title: Among the untamed / dee Hobsbawn-Smith.
Names: Hobsbawn-Smith, Dee, author.
Description: Poems.
Identifiers: Canadiana (print) 20230189679 | Canadiana (ebook) 20230189695 | ISBN 9781989466469
   (softcover) | ISBN 9781989466568 (PDF)
Classification: LCC PS8615.O23 A76 2023 | DDC C811/.6—dc23

Frontenac House gratefully acknowledges the support of the Canada Council for the Arts for our publishing program. We would also like to thank the Government of Alberta Multimedia Development Fund for their support of our publishing program.

 Canada Council   Conseil des Arts   *Alberta* Government
for the Arts   du Canada

Printed and bound in Canada
Published by Frontenac House Ltd.
37 Westridge Crescent
Okotoks, AB T1S 0G7
Tel: 403-263-7025

frontenachouse.com

Contents

Unfamiliar letters written in the foam
Jeanne Dark contemplates the prairie sky   10
Mirrored   11
Fledgling   12
Sharing Mason jars   13
That night at Mountain Mecca   14
Curatives for morning sickness   15

Bearing witness is not enough
Jeanne Dark leaves the sheltered corner   18
Where stones gather   19
Departure   20
Sounding a winter morning   22
Lines of lamentation   23
Jeanne Dark's fear of bridges   24
Orpheus enters the underworld   25
Jeanne Dark embraces the shadows   26
Marilyn (un)dressed   27
Cassandra the seer   28
Quotidian, female   31
Sty   32
Jeanne Dark enlists an army   33
Consider the bus driver   34
The Only   35
Mourning mothers   36
Jeanne Dark wages war   37
Jeanne Dark's full disclosure: a haibun   38
Amelia, vanished   40

Jeanne Dark comes of age on the prairie
Jeanne Dark comes of age on the prairie   42

The birthmother of yourself
After crossing the great divide   64
Where Jeanne Dark comes from   65
How to change the world   66
Faith-writing in the dark   67

Acknowledgements   68
Publication Credits   70
Notes   72

For the women of my family.

"Consciousness walks across the land bridge of the deer's stare into the world of things. This is knowing. It tastes of sorrow and towering appetite."
~ Tim Lilburn, *Living In The World As If It Were Home*

Jeanne Dark contemplates the prairie sky

i. Last night's sky a cauldron where heavy weather brewed, memories
black ashes gritty against the north wind –

in her dream, on a beach where dreamers boarded white sloops
bearing the newly dead to the world's edge, she saw herself embarking.

Stars trickled into a cup of clarity
until she too filled with the infinity of release.

ii. Dark warrior-woman in a dark time, she trusts her inheritance –
lives and visions of the women who came before,

her origins grounded in their world and wisdom. Her ancestors
bound by dreamscape and soil, embodied within

her feet each morning as she runs the sand hills,
her hands each afternoon as she weeds, harvests, cooks,

her bones as she lifts children, pens, knives, needles and spades.
She cherishes the dream-women as her legacy. Their invitation to her –

to desire the past's lessons, today's tempered yearnings, all
she hopes may yet be. To synthesize hurts and truths

until she blooms
into her best and truest self.

iii. This morning's sun halo strips her clean, asks
what this woman finally wants –

a simpler song, a garden to sow
and harvest, full jars on the shelves,

handmade quilt on the bed, her beloved beside her,
sons safely grown, a green field for her final sleep. Bury her

in linen embossed with cerise, malachite, forget-me-not blue
where lilacs and cherries rest nodding heads.

Two orange orioles alight on the apple bough,
flickering colour of joy after anger finally burns away.

Mirrored
~ After "What it Tastes Like" by Sheri Benning, from *Full Moon Psalm*.

It could be your grandmother – your mother, your aunt –
facing you in the glass.

Where is that young bear-mother of the photograph
protecting her young with a gaze that won't flinch,

half pain and half insurgent urge to confront?
Where is that fearless rider who cambered a wild careen

over high fences on a horse's back? Who thrust her head
into stands of poplar branches without second thoughts?

Who flung her heart forward to mark her coming across rock
walls into voids forecast by thunderclouds?

Aging, you discover the battery recharge of sunlit naps, walk sometimes
instead of running.

You miss youth's wild surfing energy,
its unbiddable surge.

Even its ebb carried a swirl of change to shore.
But the neap tide brings peace,

new to you,
unfamiliar letters written in the foam.

Fledgling

Your bedroom too small, the world too large.
You've outgrown purple walls.

No reminder needed that you chose paint, wallpaper, carpet.
Your mother both hawk and dove, father all hawk.

The rain never falls. Snow always falls.
You want a monsoon after this blizzard.

Fields are no substitute for people.
Only poems and birdsongs are written in fields.

Roast beef, gravy, mashed potatoes, always the same.
Green alfalfa makes you long to throw away your innocence.

Birdsong, no, never boring, magpie feather tangled in your hair.
But too much prairie, too much sky.

Grid roads last forever, too much gravel, the horizon too far.
Sky implies long distances and blues you can't capture or cure on paper.

Air oscillates between skunk and new-cut hay.
Stories invented by cities you want to know.

Rain washed the sky last night.
You pegged it to the clothesline to capture the thought –

Sultry saxophones, trumpets, cornets, not high lonesome fiddles.
City streetlights, tarmac, endless streams of what might be.

Women in Burkina Faso don't know how to read.
Toddlers starve in Mumbai.

Murdered tuskless elephants lie rotting in the Congo.
You want to turn your hand to helping.

Eat panang curry, pho, bulgogi.
Learn how to make linguini carbonara, mojitos, tapenade.

You'll never miss your mother. Your Daddy.
Time is a chariot across the sky. Birds fill your eyes.

Collect their feathers, their risky faith in the unknown.
Fly! For every fallen Icarus, a host of airborne women.

Sharing Mason jars
~ for Phyllis McCord

Skins slip through fingers like years
as we peel peaches at your sink,

hands quick and careful, syrup boiling, star
anise and twirls of lemon zest afloat.

Carefully we slide fruit slices
through open glass mouths,

share the day, peaches, jokes
about the lover we shared as well

with decades in between, jars and lives aligned
in the clear sunlight. You married him –

each time he walks through the kitchen we are laughing.
Bewilderment flickers through his eyes from me to you.

Linking arms, we pour cream into each other's coffee,
admire how we have contained summer, that lights

what only women know –
our friendships transcend marriage vows.

That night at Mountain Mecca

Your first date, your new man picked you up in a battle cruiser
about the same vintage as the *Millennium Falcon*
but half as flight-worthy, back seat crammed with buddies
claiming bragging rights over hooking up the two of you.

He took you to listen to Billy Cowsill, still alive, still belting it out
from the front of the band, guitars and drums,
pedal steel and accordion sweet and driving behind him,
that ramshackle floor cratering, slipping

out of true along the lino's edges where it met the crooked walls,
barbecue pit cranking out smoke-licked ribs and pulled pork to cry over,
whole place shaking with certainty that none of us
would live forever, so we'd best get on with it.

Billy burst into "Vagabond" and the dance floor filled again,
couples clutching each other, holding back the suspicion
of what might await, the night train, the fears, the shakes, the loneliness.
Pulled out of the hard streets of Vancouver

by his friends, propped up and cleaned up and dried out again,
Billy sure could sing, all that junk, heroin and booze, uppers
and downers carrying straight into the melody, a direct line
from Hank Williams and Janis Joplin, sounding out

all those lost and lonely times we knew and feared,
places we trusted Billy to shout out so we wouldn't have to.
They cut the album that night, and the whole city claimed
to have been there. You were. The band didn't tour, and Billy died –

young, as expected. We want to outlive our bad boys and heroes,
to mourn what we lost, what we didn't become.
He and you stopped dancing together. The Mecca burnt down.
He married and you moved on. Just like the song.

Curatives for morning sickness
~ For Madhur Anand

Your GP, your naturopath, thinking only *healthy baby*,
will insist on ancient sacred foods – small fish, their roe,
bone marrow, liver, the irony of eggs, raw milk.

But you have a dragon-tail to ride for nine long months.
Those moments when the whipcrack of that tail
send your innards into outer space, what then?

For then, crystallized ginger's pungent breath,
its silver threads fine silk for saris.
Nibble one piece at a time or by the handful.

Drink tea steeped with fennel. The Greeks call fennel *marathon*,
after the fennel-covered plain where the Athenians triumphed.
Childbirth is like that long run.

More licorice-loving herbs for your health –
anise seed, basil, tarragon the tiny-toothed French firedrake,
holy basil, sacred to mothers,

and star anise, steeped star of darkness,
startling brown axles and pin-wheeling heart,
figure-skating queen of spices.

Eat smoked haddock in cream,
finnan haddie to the outliers, for strength, for fortitude,
your life an island as you gestate this child.

More tea – spearmint, green tracery of hope on its leaves.
Peppermint, blue for faith – the magicking of a baby's body
within yours makes faith imperative, a given.

Drink Guinness.
For more strength.
Labour is well-named.

Eat raw mango, cook with curry leaves.
Collect hand-ground stardust,
harvested in the Outer Nebulae.

Listen. Labour. And afterwards,
when her tiny innards ride the dragon,
give her gripe water scented with licorice.

BEARING WITNESS IS NOT ENOUGH

Jeanne Dark leaves the sheltered corner

i. Each day, tea while she walks to greet sunrise in the living sky.
She looks down that long road leading away –

to what lies beyond horizon and ditch,
what wind conceals.

Even in her protected life, she hears
those unknown silent lives – and realizes

bearing witness is not enough.
Give voice to the speechless.

ii. She casts potent lines of ink
around the globe to capture evil,

links arms with other women,
female steel to stem cruelty.

iii. She watches friends knit and wear pink pussy hats in marches,
takes her sewing needle to task, stitches resolve

and fortitude into crazy patches on her husband's jeans,
creates quilts to comfort and protect, pieces

tote bags to contain fears, clothes to bring joy. Puts her knives
to use, takes pleasure in feeding all

at her table, teaches her sons to cook, to listen, to see, to reach out
hands of peace. She votes. Dissents. Argues. Defends.

iv. She speaks the names of all those lost
women and girls, none forgotten.

Where stones gather

For months, you dream the same dream – a walk
across frozen fields behind your November-coloured dog.

He ranges across blue ice and beaten-down grasses, skirts
wolf willows, orange rosehips, stands of aspen.

Where stones gather on the ridge
he rousts a skunk, dances away

to run crazy joy-rings. Then the sky flinches, two dull echoes,
and the dog leaps one last time,

blood showing on his fur. When you find him,
edge close enough to see his muzzle, young teeth exposed

to the sky, the coyotes have already come and gone,
leaving behind a framework.

The gun clatters onto rock, fallen
from unseen hands beside your dog's remains,

bones and coat of that leaping animal reduced
to gristle and one white paw.

Departure

Cain cannot remember life
without the sound of paws padding beside him,
two dogs, gifts from Adam as pups.

Both cringe now, blood splatters disfiguring
the white coat of one. Teeth bared, whining, they ignore
Cain's repeated whistle, slink away when he turns east.

Above him, the whisper of wings, wind a warning
as geese rabble southward in a ragged squadron.
Exile begins.

The rock he used lodges
within his chest. When he finally falls
into sleep, hand splayed to cover its stain, his dream lands

feet-first in Eden's orchard, but pear and pomegranate turn
to shale and blood between his clenched fingers.
Awake, he stops counting his footfalls, learns

the true measure of Eden by distance travelled
away, a trail of seeds marking
his route. Hears footpads, toenails clicking

on rock, but no floppy ears appear
when he calls. That night he builds his first fire.
Yellow eyes beyond its reach.

He spends a day searching, piles rocks
beside the embers, heaves them
at the yellow eyes in the night. Skins the wolf next day

with stones he sharpens, scraping
one over the other. Slings the skin, still dripping,
over his shoulders where it hardens around him.

In the night he searches again
for yellow eyes, listens for padding paws.
Is this loneliness?

Cain's grasses and seeds fall from his hand. No orchards here,
no arbours for shelter. He grows lean and hard, at night
his own fist rasping against his sex like sand on rock.

He dreams again of the raven scratching
at the soil, as he himself scratched out
a burial plot. His dead brother

visits him each night, arriving in a hail
of grain and pulses, emmer and lentil falling
from his skin like blessings. They bring no blessings,

for Cain wakes hungry each day, pulls wrinkled roots
from beneath his feet, gnawing, always gnawing, never
satisfied. How to endure?

The dead will never stride again
into the flocks, nor offer up
the fattest lamb to the family meal.

Regret an arroyo that leads to an abandoned garden.
He stops weeping when the tears bake into salt
cracking his unshaven cheeks.

What can memory offer save more mourning?
In centuries distant, brothers will still slay brothers
and mothers mourn children.

He knows salt will be sown
in the fields he left behind, rubbing injustice
into every mote of soil. A woman will be pilloried and stoned.

He knows this too, and that children will be murdered
on bleeding beaches. Waking dreams drive him forward
into unknown lands, no paws padding at his heels.

Sounding a winter morning

Snow crunches underfoot, crystal teeth biting
at the road's edge, empty

of anything but frettings,
those staccato violin notes.

Grain truck a mile away, tires and engine moan
along the frozen gravel road.

Double strand of wool unwinds behind a jet,
the growl of it unfurling two white breaths later.

Train filled with barley ten miles distant
whistles to clouds as if they were errant calves.

Chickadees in the willows remind each other
of an upcoming tea party. Sparrows chatter

in the pole barn, metal roof amplifying
conversation into argument.

Yelps unite into a single coyote voice
piercing the sky like a nail into timber.

In its wake, a telegraph trail of howls
across the horizon from unseen dogs

who catch the vibe, articulating
what you didn't know you needed to say.

Lines of lamentation

Her wedding dress a pelican with sails for wings. Silk feathers
for his bowtie, sunflower petals blown free from her hair, his boutonniere.

Confusion after his phone call announcing her departure: Send out notices
of revocation? Issue an anti-marriage writ? Summon the banshee wails

of the sidhe? Offer comfort or congratulations? This mourning,
no peace in your lifetime, kittens going blindly to distemper.

This is lonely brothers, Cain calling
in his mourning voice for Abel.

This cold soup congealed in a northeast wind. Solitary
goose. Spilled tea, broken teapot.

A raven a crow a magpie, voices awry like cracked winter, fallen
feathers drowned in mud, corvid cement caught in your throat.

This wind. Coyotes spinning tops. Basement floods and rivers run amok.
Barn walls clanging, metal skin on metal struts.

Trees bent flat. This is Paxil, Prozac, snapped bone
snagged in shredded cloth. This is forgotten cars gone to rust.

Your former mother-in-law lonely in long-term care,
a basement's slitted eyes.

Unscratch soft names from hard rocks: schist, moraine, loess, limestone,
fieldstone. This is the cave and no thread to unwind. Lost vowels. Hard

consonants. The black hound won't be comforted, familiar
unwelcome uncle.

Migrating geese gone silent, ducks mourning in a minor key.
Magpie nest, an abandoned clutter of twigs. Remember

all the white magic of that early pelican sighting. Gather one feather,
shedding raindrops in a glorious sheet. Your brother's tobacco tin, a lighter.

Listen for one goose calling, and strike flint to the pirate sky.
Galleons and oars of light hover just beyond the horizon.

Jeanne Dark's fear of bridges

In the Canadian Rockies, Golden Gorge falls away beneath concrete pillars,
a steep cut through the nothingness of a mountain pass.

Near San Francisco, San Rafael bridge arcs between
bay and sky, touches down in Marin County.

Port Mann bridge crosses the Fraser River from Vancouver, creeping cars
buffeted by rain and shadows of semi-trailers under misted cables.

She grits her teeth. Looks only at the road
in front of the windshield. Another –

Calgary's Centre Street bridge: she once
saw a teenaged girl cross its underbelly, just her

and a backpack, yesterday's skirt, black Docs, a tattoo
on her arm half-visible – a totem of an owl.

But its wisdom hadn't taken root – there the girl stood,
alone under the bridge at dusk.

As she drove by, two men approached. Only the divided
boulevard kept her from wheeling around to rattle them away.

Told herself maybe they were cops, come to do a good turn
for a homeless kid. But maybe not.

Saw the girl again still shadowed by men
at the shelter where she served supper.

Later, after she left, the girl stood again under the bridge.
Still wishes she'd gathered her up to safety.

Told herself, *You can't
save them all.* As if that excused letting her go.

Orpheus enters the underworld

What if the path to the river is snowbound?
What if the ice bridge is thrown down? What if frosted javelins
barrage the air? If the great guard dog turns
his night-stained muzzle and roars?

What if the way is a black and white Polaroid,
trees and ground frozen mid-thought? If even that dog
is brindled landscape, black blurring
into grey, grey into white?

What if she doesn't follow?
What if not even the stones speak?
If every pebble echoes and the caverns
are shadowed by burning torches that gutter and hiss?

What if the soil mutinies, turns
to mud, to muskeg, to mould?
What if you lie down in exhaustion?
What if the ice thickens your voice into croak?

What if she can no longer see you?
If your tortoiseshell lyre cracks?
If your strings break?
If she doesn't want to leave?

Jeanne Dark embraces the shadows

She examines the dim edges where, in the shades, linger
her past mistakes and the damages she wrought.

Along their rippled memory she spies the ley lines that might be
chance, what she sees as possibility –

how a man may still embrace a woman,
how a child may yet grow strong,

how some women choose women, how liminal spaces offer
choice. How dawn follows darkness.

In the shadows dwell those unspoken nodes
that might blossom into spines and prickles

of conscience, night-blooming cacti of discomfort
that bring a desert into bloom.

Marilyn (un)dressed

Beside you in the museum gallery, a teenaged mother-girl,
halter top tied over generous tattoos, audacity

in her sideways grin at a row of famous dresses
adorning dressmakers' dummies. She exclaims over glowing taffeta

and silk, lush velvet. You wonder out loud about breasts,
Marilyn's no larger than what hides beneath your t-shirt.

More than clothes created that aura, goddess-lore spilling
beyond the celluloid image, his hands on that sex-queen physique

captured in the photographer's silver sizzle, her clothing gaped at –
art, or a sideshow?

Sewn into a strapless sheath for her serenade,
imagination adds breathy details as she sings

Happy birthday, Mister President, quicksilver dress,
skin a-shimmer beneath the crushing weight of crystals.

(Un)dressed for *The Seven Year Itch*, white skirt a cloud
around her legs above the subway's hot breath, neighbour man entranced,

building heat. Her stage-name and sex-goddess image a stone albatross,
finally coldcocks her, newspapers agog

with salacious details of her death alone,
eyelids canopied over luminous blue eyes, invitation shuttered.

Fashion mannequins and video dance-queens mirror her sexuality
on catwalks and online, monetized, weaponized, glamour all hard

surfaces, lacking the softnesses that made Marilyn human, frail
as you, as tattooed teen's teething baby smiling

in a rattletrap stroller, small hands reaching
for the comfort of breasts. Leave the gallery more vulnerable,

cherish women's seasons – the child still maiden, then divinely
ripened breasts and hips, finally an elder's clear vision.

You inhabited the goddess role briefly before your season
passed. She never lived past full-blown rose.

Cassandra the seer
~ After the 1895 marble bust by Max Klinger, Musée d'Orsay, Paris

i. Within my ears the bells of the universe toll the deaths
of all I know – my city, my brothers, my own.
The bells announce our lives from birth to passing,
fabric woven from sound, warp and weft resonating into the future.

Within my ears the past and yet to come –
cracking walls, fires, soldiers bent on brutality, my city falling
into antiquity, to be re-found in a century
I cannot imagine –

as treasure uncovered spoonful by spoonful,
revealing our walls, golden urns, the masks of our conquerors.
Nowhere will be found the lyre, tuned
to the key of the heavens, that sounded only for me.

ii. My marble eyes cloaked,
a hood of clay protects me.
I was cursed, doomed to walk a corridor set with many windows
onto eternal night, cursed to know

when I breathed in the light from the temple garden for the last time,
when I stood above my city, upraised arms ignored,
when I said what must be said despite the deafness all around,
when I told the death-hours before they were rung.

Apollo's vengeance – his temple snakes curled against me
found my neck, my armpit,
then both ears, slithering tongues
clearing out all static, the resonances yet to come

amplifying in my head like clappered bells.
It drove me mad. So the soothsayers claimed, ousted
from their spot at the Trojan royal table,
usurped by the King's red-haired sprig

with voices in her head. It was they who sowed the seed
of stigma, rumouring Apollo's favour was granted, then denied
when I denied him my body, a woman's prerogative, yes, but that gained me
a god's revenge – to know, to be heard, but disbelieved.

iii. I heard Death before it came to Hector, the sword's hiss
as it opened my brother to the dogs,
the pop of tendons severed,
the chariot's creak as Achilles hauled his corpse around Troy's walls.

Enough to keep me in the world of madness,
in the rape of war. *Beware of horses,* I said.
Madness, they answered, *she's mad,
just look at her eyes.*

It took no insurgent Trojan Horse,
no fires, no falling walls,
to crack the glazed clay of my eyes.
My own end, I already knew: rape in Athena's temple,

a half-life as slave, concubine, and in a far-off land, to die,
seeing the axe-blade fall before it
    fells me.
All-seeing eyes, ears that hear, O treacherous tongue,

unbelieved. My world spins to its end,
and no one listens.

iv. How many words for pain? for loss?
Draw your rope ladders up after you, bind your wounds –
peace is a foreign land worth visiting.
War comes, I tell you this. I tell you.

How many dead? Numbers beyond counting,
bodies of babies drowned in the sea, lost women, ravaged men.
A jungle razed, a town bombed. Death
by radiation, by orange fire blossoms, by insensate drones.

War comes! Bind up your wounds. Bind them,
and bind yourself to the mast, again we sail toward war
and again, no one attends to my words.
Draw up your ladders. Listen! Do you hear me?

Within my head, the raging voices,
temples fallen upon me, snakes sinister,
and none to listen. Bind up your dead, bind up
the jaws of Hector. Peace is a foreign ... none shall heed.

v. Lost among other warnings,
another small girl, solitary in her tent,
looks into the dead faces of her parents, seeing only sky
where war rides on the backs of drones,

alone in her fear of what lurks outside the walls – the road to Death
entirely imaginable. The warnings,
nightly on the six o'clock news, repeated at ten. Peace is ....
Still you don't heed me.

Quotidian, female

On a bus in New Delhi. On pig farms in Canada. On the Highway of Tears. In deserts, squares. On beaches. In Vancouver's Downtown Eastside doorways. Needles and cocks rammed into them. On the bus, even the driver takes a turn.

On the barren Yellowhead Highway, eighteen young Indigenous women gone, hitchhikers.

On a farm in Port Coquitlam, BC. Bones, skeletons, teeth, a revolver fitted with a dildo, faux-fur-lined handcuffs, a syringe. Twenty-seven murdered women. Eighteen statements read by the prosecutor:[1]

"If the teardrops I shed made a pathway to heaven, I would walk all the way."[2]

In St. Catherine's, Ontario, three girls drugged, raped, murdered by a woman and her husband. Valium-spiked spaghetti. Halcion. An electrical cord, a mallet and a homemade video. One was her sister.

In Cleveland, Ohio, three girls abducted, raped, beaten into miscarriages, childbirth. Their lives, humanity, dignity, their child-bearing ability, all disposable, valueless to their captor. No amber alert, imprisoned in a basement for a decade. A six-year-old child rescued with them.

In Ciudad Juarez, Mexico, over two decades, two hundred and sixty Latina girls and women raped, mutilated, murdered, bodies abandoned in the desert to rot.

In Madan Chak, Pakistan, two teenaged girls raped, then shot to death, and a child sodomized and murdered, her body dumped on a Karachi beach.

Near Mumbai, India, a four-year-old girl raped by a cleaner wanting to show her some tricks. In Weifang, China, a gifted student raped, smothered, dismembered, abandoned by her teacher. Her family left with only a lock of her hair.

In Tahrir Square, Egyptian women and foreign journalists raped. One hundred and sixty-nine in one week. "We call it the circle of hell."[3]

More before, more since. So many. Too many.

Sty

Your mother warned on every visit, *Don't let your boy
into the sty alone.*

Years later, you see
farrowing sows, wide bloated bellies

sailing for their suckling offspring,
and doubt what she'd said. Until the radio

unleashes reports, all those missing mangled women,
and you see again those sows' teeth

snort through the trough, recall
the slickness of pigskin gloves, worn daily

to protect your hands, toughness that you love
stained with horse sweat and soil, never

thought once about the chops grilling
late at night for dinner.

Weeping for the women
as you push away the plate.

Jeanne Dark enlists an army

Some moments, after reading the onscreen news,
she succumbs.

Evil seems endless after so many centuries, so many deaths.
So many lost women. The why of it eludes her.

How to alter the course of such profound loss?
Staring in the mirror, she rallies, calls her friends.

They meet. Hugs shared, wine poured, coffee and cake
to follow. Together they climb and fall, regain their feet, over and over,

clamber up that hill, arm themselves with love, with the spirit
of wholeness, with kindness, with hands tempered by strong justice.

Consider the bus driver

She prefers to imagine him alone with his rearview mirror,
rows of empty benches and all-seeing windows
bearing witness, his seat a backless stool,
its spring uncoiling, corkscrewed metal
impaling him.

This, the only form of punishment
she can rely on to allay
the way his hands unsheathed themselves,
the coiling ligature of fingers, the lines he left
along her throat and thighs.

She sees the stool, a steel spring
motionless, its penetrating
column emerging
from his mouth, as justice
she may never otherwise find.

The Only

i. On a rare trip to town, your father takes you to The Only
for fish and chips, skid row, Downtown Eastside,
Vancouver's underbelly showing itself white as cod
before the battering hides its pale dead gleam.

Safe in your booth, you are afraid
to look for a bathroom, what teenage eyes might find.
There ain't one, girlie, the cook belches past his smoke, and you twist
your legs together on the red naugahyde bench,

ignore the stench of piss coming in waves
through the front door, watch the grizzled cook's bare arms
carve apart a cod, hook half a halibut from the white chipped ice, slice it
open, tidy steaks and fillets falling from his blade,

big knife alive in his tattooed hands.
Your father cranes long arms and legs past you to observe
the parade outside, faces of transgenders and child sex workers
blued beneath The Only's neon seahorse sign.

ii. At 23, you return alone – caught on the memory
of that cook's meaty hands as he carved up the fish –
past Carnegie Centre, the back alleys where needles cluster,
drowned dreams in the rain, to seventeen stools still spinning

crazy at the counter beneath the blue seahorse.
Sheltered at the stained Formica, cigarette smouldering
while the same cook nudges his knuckles
through a sea of clams. Behind you the shadow

of your father's arms holds the door
to the street and those abandoned girls,
the colour of suffering shining
in the shadows like that cod belly.

Mourning mothers

All spring you watch the barn-cats grow gourd-shaped, swell
with the garden rains. Even Essie, a yearling too tiny
for motherhood. And she is,
miscarries her kits.

In summer kittens, hiding in hay, emerge
when you aren't watching, sleep in the sun,
cavort on coil-spring hocks and whipcord heels, then scattershot,
vanish when you approach.

Their mothers greet you each morning, a welcome wagon
of feline hunger, high-tailed nursing
mamas tangled beneath your feet.
You befriend their babies, name them all –

Cantucci, Biscotti and Befanini, Baci – their sister,
Anginetta, Amaretto – blind in one eye,
Tozetti and Torrone – one solid and one pied,
a dozen kittens all sweet as cookies.

One fall morning they're gone.
Six mamas haunt you with plaintive voices
while you hang clothes on the line, pull the last carrots, watch
mergansers and coots tip tails up in the lake.

Listening to the evening news, you imagine
all the ways death can vanish
a clutch of kittens
as easily as women and girls.

Red-tailed hawk on cruise control.
Great horned owl, deadly smoke at night.
Perennially hungry skunk, omnivorous. Coyotes
on the perimeter of the lake. Men bearing brown bags or weapons.

No bodies to bury. No evidence, no certainty.
No cantor, no kaddish.
No males to weep with you.
Just mourning mothers.

Jeanne Dark wages war

In decades when she abandons her body's kinetic knowledge.

In years of the hot forge, among incandescent flames she does not understand but only lives by.

In the line of knives she learns to leave lying in moments of anger, double-edged bevels that would unmake them both.

In grief hardening around ribs and heart, rage calcifying into granite.

In the sandstone grit of resentment.

In the vanguard of black-sail clouds, corsairs of fury.

In moments of pure hatred, visceral open-heart surgery, closing valves and blocking arteries.

In white heat of thrown fists and recriminations.

In implacable needs of her body, sex a weapon, not a bridge.

In the seductive moat of wine, drawbridge lowered long enough for an onslaught of arrows, a torrent of javelins, daggers aimed at each other's heart.

In the wild abandon of wrath, aftermath's exhaustion.

Until her awareness that retreat is no victory.

Finis. Eventually
    détente.

Jeanne Dark's full disclosure: a haibun

i. Too young to worry when the blacksmith heated the torch for the first time. *Stop it,* she wanted to shriek with the calves at branding, *STOP IT NOW*. But she closed her mouth around his cock and swallowed. First mistake. The next: caught in the forge, cozened like a filly without protest. Wanting to soften his hand on the hammer, she told herself she let him.

New moon honours loss –
mourns early vernal blood-flow
you the willing lamb

ii. Decades later she learned how touch pays tribute to obsession. A voice in the dark. Escarpment of knees, hands, ribcage. And footprints on the wall afterwards, smeared oil marking her climb. Heat surging. His birdlike half-dance, courting her. Walking to the outhouse naked, aware he watched through the jungle garden, cedars, unkempt rhododendrons, blackberry brambles, bamboo. They snatched days and weeks, rarely slept, talked by the half-lit moon, breakers crashing beyond the window while the list of what they didn't discuss grew longer. In the end, even poetry radiated the energy of *verboten*. All they had was fire. All that's left is ash. She writes letters sporadically, as if to a benevolent uncle, of dogs cats weather lakes meals friends makings. The *verboten* list longer now.

Island's new moon tide –
berries crushed beneath your hip
words grit   fallen ash

iii. After fucking, time as translucent as stretched taffy. When the veil thins – on the peninsula jutting into the lake, a goose rears back, immense wings fold, unfold. Dog chews a stick. Sleepy bees buzz, ragged squadron of ducks practice late-summer lift-off. The squadron breaks, reforms when the drill sergeant harangues. One *quack*.

Honeybee on sunflower –
gold on gold petals   tremble
pollen in the breeze

iv. Coyotes harmonize, chorale in a dozen voices, pups' sopranos soaring and yipping above adult altos and tenors. Her dogs lift their muzzles to the sky and answer, unexpected trills and warbles issuing from their deep chests. The serenade stops her each evening. Calling geese form patrols and fly, primal response a mysterious sexual attraction. Sing back to the sky, magic at its best. At its worst, sweaty nights and guilt. Letters mailed in regret, letters not sent.

Coyote calls your name –
trickster pads into the yard
solstice-yellow eyes

v. Her friend's emailed pregnancy journal continues: *There's pleasure in telling a secret.* She's forgotten that pleasure, chocolate melting in the mouth. What has she taken pleasure in disclosing? She danced, a dervish in the garden, when she told a girlfriend about her secret lover, her whirling hair a compass back to him.

Shared honeysuckle –
blooms for lovers' sworn secrets
unnamed in public

vi. The end, hot and bitter – the reek of stressed metal in her mouth when she leaves him. She wishes the blacksmith had never touched her, never branded her. Affairs always end like this, a doom of bitter tastes and burning that bring back hot memories of his forge.

Amelia, vanished

In the drowned grove a black bird roosts,
snowy head and tail-feathers, stevedore's shoulders.
Bigger than a buteo, unfamiliar. Your guesses settle
with a rattle of wings: a juvenile bald eagle.

When you return, the visitor is gone.
But one feather blazes from the black tree and you remember
Amelia who flew off the radar screens,
burned her way through life, the sky her flame.

She took off in a wooden box from the toolshed roof,
bruises and compulsion blooming simultaneously,
dive-bombed by a flying ace in a red stubble-jumper,
the wings' enticing whisper as he cruised by.

Cropped her hair, bought a leather bomber jacket,
a flying cap, her first plane, climbed that Canary
higher than any woman before, solo
across the Atlantic. Famous flyer,

years later nothing came between her and her Electra
until Howland Island emerged from clouds,
a black stump in the Pacific.
One thousand feet above the waves, low on fuel,

deaf to radio transmissions, blind
to smoke plumes from the *Itasca*, anchored
off the island. Two weeks of searching found only legend.
Not even a feather left behind.

JEANNE DARK COMES OF AGE ON THE PRAIRIE

Jeanne Dark comes of age on the prairie

i.
Stuck in the middle
of open space somewhere[1]

my only companions the restless winds with airsong names –
Chinook, Mistral, Cers, Foëhn, Santana, Harmattan, Sirocco –
winds the only music, polishing snow into crystals,
scratching hieroglyphics on stone, etching sand
into dunes, skiffling poplar leaves
and riverwater into whitecaps. Only the winds answer,
their ciphers more enigmatic than the oracles,
why it takes so long to learn the mariner's compass,
true north of the soul always dyed
a darker indigo than death. On this breeze rides the possibility
of what to (be)come, couched in the mutable
language of spirit, the whistle of excitement that marks creation:
be the goddess-queen draped in green amber, in green vines,
in green leaves, the birthmother of yourself.

---

1 William Robertson, "Father" from *Standing on My Own Two Feet* (Coteau, 1986).

ii.
The woman who pierces
flesh for a living snaps[2]

the strap of my camisole
out of her way. A tattooed dragon's tooth
and jaw can't be stopped
by a simple line of stitchery, by cotton pulled snug, any more
than a poem can be halted
by a gale gusting into the forest.
Each recedes, re-gathers, again surges into breath.
Her fingers are sure, stained
with ochre and sienna and cinnabar and umber and crimson
fading to vermilion sunlight
as she sketches a lucid line that transforms
into eyes, patient incisors, willful jaws.
What emerges in the mirror is the dragon within,
awaiting the invitation to reveal herself.

---

2   Belinda Betker, "Pierce" from *Fast Forward: New Saskatchewan Poets* (Hagios, 2007).

iii.
The best part of a man
is a woman, her softnesses[3]

they said, but how hard I struggled to strap that softness
into steel, using strips torn from my imagination

to bind myself into a semblance
of masculinity, concealing small breasts beneath

tomboy tunics, denying monthly bloodflow, staunching
stains and returning to the saddle like a Knight Templar

intent on defending the Holy City, before I learned
the Holy City hidden within, before my garden – riotous cornflowers,

columbines, clematis and poppies, larkspur and sunflowers – took root,
no scent of a woman yet unleashed. All I knew was the hard line

of my abdominal muscles, taut calves, limber thighs, as I struggled
to reproduce a masculine form in my lithe frame years before

children and childbirth, grace and surrender, widened my stance,
the divinity of the feminine not yet my goal, born a girl by mistake.

---

[3] Dave Margoshes, "Adam's Rib" from *Purity of Absence* (Dundurn, 2001).

iv.
If I turn very quickly
I can just catch her moving[4]

that *her* I've grown into and barely recognize
in the mirror, that *her*, a composite of all the women

who've come before me: my aunt's wayward
grin and blowsy hair, my mother's narrowing

eyes that view miles of prairie as her privilege to safeguard,
my grandmother's broad brow and cheekbones echoing

another place and era, my sister's anxious hand-flutter
so like our grandmother's it smudges time. Within them all,

embroidered upon their lives like bolts of embossed bouclé tossed wild
upon the wind, I see myself,

variegated vine that climbs and entwines,
no separating me from them, now from then.

---

[4] Kathleen Wall, "Landscapes With Absent Figure" from *Time's Body* (Hagios, 2005).

v.
The fire dies, the cabin is black.
Here we feed the silence.[5]

The women came through time, all the women
of my line, witches and shamans and diviners and medicine women

seers who guided me to this place now feed the silence of the future
with songs of the past, and the cabin's air is amber green and crimson,

sienna and cinnabar fading to vermilion sun, serene
voices transmuting into light that can't be bound or steeled.

Tint and shade blur into ripples of cerulean blue, fishes' scales,
magpie's feathers, iridescent with possibility. What my ancestors offer

to share – miles of prairie to tend, dragons' wisdom
and new-hatched hope – may survive within another woman

draped in amber green as goddess, or queen in silver light. How a legend
leaps to life, when the winds still, when fire dies and embers flicker.

---

5 Brenda Schmidt, "Night on An Old Trade Route" from *More Than Three Feet of Ice* (Thistledown, 2005).

vi.
On the beach, I am who I imagine
I am, a boy[6]

bearing a jackknife, no, carrying a rod and reel,
no, hauling a sword and shield, no, clasping coloured pencils

and one thin book of empty pages.
I fill them one by one with leaping fish about to transform,

becoming dragons, dragonflies, hunters pursuing the hunted,
and sketch a lad narrow as a fishing rod, no curves except

as the wind cambers line into arc, tugs free from the page
the girl sheltering within, unable to resist the allure of iridescent

scales and wings – magpie, trout – that leap and skitter,
details captured shade by shining shade,

fluctuating pigments and wavering lines on sheets of paper.
What does it mean to be a girl?

---

6   Elizabeth Philips, "Jackknife/1" from *Torch River* (Brick, 2007).

vii.
I liked myself better
before I became a saint, those hours[7]

spent imagining myself as Joan of Arc – Joan
of curves? Of shadows? Wasted time in either case.

Warrior-girl, androgyne, clad in dragon-tattooed chain
mail and helmet, hair cut in a blunt bowl, all lean legs

and fire-clenching arms, the ardour of conversion lighting my face
before two armies. Man? Woman? Who will follow a girl?

They do not want a saint. Look at the Twitter feeds, the FaceBook
meta-pages devoted to darkness, to danger, to celebrity.

I must dive into the waters of war even though within
my armour chafes the tender parts that I, who did not wish

for them, cannot deny, never let myself feel. Even my brothers
claim they knew all along I was meant to be a boy.

---

7 Joanne Weber "Dorothy Day: Annunciation" from *The Pear Orchard* (Hagios, 2007).

viii.
He forgot one wound
in another[8]

the first time he plunged into me, clutched me close, but
I rolled free. I am no sheath for a lance. What is a woman for?

I wanted to ask as I bled on his sheets. I still do not know.
My wound retreated from the material world to where

only I could vouch for it. As breasts grew and hips spread,
as my balance shifted on my horse and my sword hand rejected

its weapon, I wanted to ask again. What is a woman for?
Spells emanate from inner spirits, ancestors urging me on,

but to what? I do not know. I dream of robes spun from iridescent
green amber and woad blue, nascent

wings that tickle my shoulder blades and itch while I sleep.

---

8 Don Kerr, "the last day" from *The Dust of Just Beginning* (Athabasca University, 2010).

ix.
at fifteen my first boyfriend
my mother saying don't disappoint me[9]

and me too dense to know what she meant as we lay together
while his family cracked ice open and fished winter into spring, silver

gleaming on snow like dreams on diamonds, frozen
filaments of fish flying into the frying pan, splattering us with butter

generous as wishes, my stained sweater transforming in the firelight
into green amber and lapis lazuli blue as I imagined

what kind of woman I might be
when I left behind the ice floes of teen years.

---

9   Lynda Monahan, "what she must never do" from *what my body knows* (Coteau, 2003).

x.
As a child she tried on churches
like ladies' hats,[10]

my sister reported that they all pinched, both of us caught
in wooden pews bereft of cushions, tethered rowboats bound to wharves,

so we wandered from the church's shore, she and I, looked to the skies
and to the creek, to the woods where small fires burned at night,

where killdeer and avocets slept, only the owls asking who.
I shed robe and vestments, and took up the raiment

of the blessed and now walk among the untamed, to ask the wild ones
in their many tongues how to be a woman. The untamed things cast

many answers on the wind, words lost before the green amber oak leaves
fall umber in its current. As aging crimson oak leaves turn

before the storm, and dwindling, fade to ochre
within the storm's heart, I listen

shelter each leaf in my hands, a gem, and wonder,
but I have no answer.

---

10 dee Hobsbawn-Smith, "Embolism" from *Wildness Rushing In* (Hagios, 2014).

xi.
Ride off any horizon
and let the measure fall[11]

I hear the Chinook wind cry one afternoon, waking
curiosity for what lies beyond

the miles of prairie my mother's eye blessed. The time has come
to ride. The melody hovers as I pack – handful of green amber dust,

pinch of aurora borealis, spun starlight set with silver filament,
the moon's first hint of burnt umber.

I ride into an arc so clear
my teeth ache. When I look up into eyes as blue,

as deep, as the flax seeds gathering force in my mother's cupboard,
as wide as the hips I dreamed myself into,

I begin to understand.

---

11 John Newlove, "Ride Off Any Horizon" from *A Long Continual Argument* (Chaudiere, 2007).

xii.
you got talking
just because[12]

those blue eyes. Just. Because. All the things my mother warned.
Tell myself be cautious, be careful. Be here now, now.

We get to talking and before I know to say please or thank you, he's packing
my things into a carryall I never see again,

tosses them over his shoulder – my dewlight and early
morning solo dances, my late-night borealis

glow, my green amber dust – left
with only the amber spikes within his irises. They fade to gray,

and I am bereft, empty as a torn pocket, betrayer wind howling
and piling up snow on the leeward side, crystals forming on my lakeshore

as if some ship had foundered there, ice blocks and torqueing
jacks and ice-queen stay spells rendering me

– abandoned in icy ink –
alone in winter white.

---

12   Randy Lundy, "just because" from *Under the Night Sun* (Coteau, 1999).

xiii.
Karaoke never paid the rent
or did it? My night students ask[13]

as well they might when I shimmy around them
all hip and lip gloss, words shifting me out

of focus, *sing with me, sing,* I implore. They do,
but pity takes tonal control and song goes sour – The Band

on a bad night, Robbie Robertson gone home, Levon loaded, Dylan
forever offkey. Crazy dreams, what's left of my madhouse

life, a northern township with no road out, no ice
bridge, spring's unreliable melts become songs flickering on the wall

with my night students' wan and fading voices. Is this all there is?
Then let's dance. The ice queen calls.

---

13 Jeanette Lynes, "Abba Down Cold" from *A Woman Alone on the Atikokan Highway* (Wolsak & Wynn, 1999).

xiv.
The body's belief in death is simple, true, taken up
by the unwilled muscle that fills then empties the lungs[14]

and these muscles, this set of tendons sprung on bone, all unwilling to stay,
propel me through the hours, each night a jelly bean gemstone

cracking like burnt brulée, my northern tiara
tarnished, ashen with overpolishing and exposure

to the elements. What will transport me from this town – any
small town – mineshaft of a town with sunken centre

and blackened edges? I've forgotten the airsongs –
Chinook, Mistral, Cers, Foëhn, Santana, Harmattan, Sirocco –

voices silenced among Quonset huts and shafts and buried stones
roughened from mined-out green amber and dwindling raw umber,

by heaps of poison, slag the mine dredges up and leaves behind. My dream –
wildfire the colour of azure blue and burnt ochre – abandoned.

I've settled for dull olive mud that pools in a tailings pond
at my open door.

---

14 Paul Wilson, "Swept" from *Turning Mountain* (Wolsak & Wynn, 2007).

xv.
A child who is born covered
in clay & smelling of horses[15]

I forgot so much. My warrior heart bound
by what they call progress,

clay choking me,
the smell of horses buried in the future

beneath car exhaust and motor oil and diesel, singed.
Catch my breath now and I'm liable to ignite.

---

15 Katherine Lawrence, "A Gift" from *Ring Finger, Left Hand* (Coteau, 2001).

xvi.
The dog sees it
(frozen)[16]

and barks at the notion of a girl-woman
(frozen) and attempting escape.

I seek redemption, flee the truck stop, night students, karaoke bar,
my pack of ancestors ahead of me, flitting

tree to tree as I did when a child
wanting only the sureness of earth beneath my soles,

ceiling of stars above, white birch bark under my fingertips, moon
blessing me, firesong of melting amber in my ears, surrounded

by the ghosts of women
who love me, voices in the wind like arrows.

---

16   gillian harding-russell, "broad daylight" from *Vertigo* (River, 2004).

xvii.
Old as it is, it's in my house now—
come from Winnipeg on the back of a truck,[17]

far from any small-minded town where women suffer,
stoned or drudged or slaughtered, wan under azure light.

I must disable the rack-and-pinion of loneliness,
surrender the lance of fear, the armour of despair, gently remove

each bolt and plate, bathe with cornflowers and catmint blooms
until my skin remembers green amber and lapis lazuli.

---

17 Bruce Rice, "Winnipeg Couch" from *The Trouble with Beauty* (Coteau, 2014).

xviii.
The moon was gone
when Yarrow left the house[18]

and when Chamomile, Columbine and Aster,
Delphinium and Borage, Basil and Feverfew struck out

from their garden to bring their daughter home. In fever I struggle
for their names, chant their virtues, recall them from hiding,

and they wash my face with the breath of beauty
and petals of remembrance

until I walk again with the beams of sun,
moon and stars saturate my skin, lover of the light.

---

18 Robert Currie, "Returning Alone" from *Yarrow* (Oberon, 1980).

xix.
In the near dark,
when she's almost[19]

transparent, when she sees herself from a distance,
she regains her true identity, finds the breath of "I" again –

takes on the glamour of one who walked the fire and emerged
not whole, not unmarked,

wits grown deep green amber, tone gone south
like an old bell whose cracks are mended but not true,

I return to my steeple, ring deepened, shine charged
to magpie iridescent turquoise blue.

---

19 Sheri Benning, "What It Tastes Like" from *Thin Moon Psalm* (Brick, 2007).

xx.
I leave my shoes
to mark my place[20]

but their tongues have grown flutter-wings
and flown, and I am left

with feathered words to inscribe on a biddable page –
be true, my life –

and my essence rests in the basket I weave
from my mistakes, from the lives and memories of all the women,

my ancestors, my shamans, mystics and seers, my witches,
my medicine women and diviners, all those wisdoms that made me,

mosaic of dark valleys that bend into rivers, rivers that yield
to oceans, oceans that surrender to the winds.

---

20 Anne Campbell, "I Leave My Shoes to Mark My Place" from *Angel Wings All Over* (Thistledown, 1994).

THE BIRTHMOTHER OF YOURSELF

After crossing the great divide

They still call her a young river but that's just politeness. Once she crashed
downhill from the mountains, unstoppable spray

over rocks, through narrowing channels and beds. Careless
of where she thundered

rapids to waterfall to great plains. Her undercurrents swept away
levees and causeways, breached banks, washed out bridges.

Now she broadens, finds small burble-pockets, riffles into tiny cascades,
creates momentary pools of rest for the dragonflies to touch down.

A slow current towards a place of reckoning,
still unstoppable, still wild within,

called to that sandy shore
where she will merge with the sea.

Where Jeanne Dark comes from

You travel dusty roads for hours
to share hugs, a piece of pie and conversation,

and when they ask your reason
you say, *Just being neighbourly.*

No tough crusts out here, just tough cookies.
This place weeds out weaklings, dilettantes, wobblers.

Carry snow boots and shovel,
matches and candle, spare

scarves for two. Make room
for imagery beside the ice scraper and toques,

a book of poetry, novels that end
with hope. Pack kindness among the mittens.

More berries and cream, another slice?
Say yes, chat up that old beauty.

It'll be you soon enough,
you too will want a friend to visit.

How to change the world
~ for Sarah-jane Newman

i. She leaves ahead of you, hands full of embossed gift glasses. Run
to catch up, after dancing like hellions, after singing loudly,

after many toasts to bride and groom, dresses awry
with whirling and wine.

You take up the guitar at fifty, stubby fingers
struggle to fit around chords that resist your hands, play

the stuck notes for her over and over on the phone. Sing together,
sing her favourite song on her birthday, distorted

over the pandemic's glassy Zoom-face, but still you sing.
Talk daily as you walk different paths, dogs at your heels,

voices carrying over wind and static.

ii. Over coffee with her, speak your halting best in their language
to the lost travellers without local currency –

banks already closed, no ATM card, no smartphone, can't read English.
Together, take them to the hotel, give them your uneaten cake,

your theatre tickets, as someone once did for you –
Vienna, the Staatsoper, *The Nutcracker* – imprinted forever by gifts,

kindnesses of strangers on the streetcar telling you,
Ask for schnitzel, ein glas Weiss Wein, bitte, apfel strudel mit schlag.

She gives them the full wine bottle in her car.
You show them a good café.

iii. Send her photos of periwinkle-blue flax fields
so she can paint the prairie sky's reflection.

Bring her to the wild meadow, the first silk-strewn pasque flower,
Easter crocus, anemone, grey and mauve

prairie smoke that also may endure the years.

Faith-writing in the dark

i. Recall what the dream asked you to give up –
chocolate, tea, coffee, lemon cake, red wine,

your body as you once knew it.
In the mirror, your shape a stranger,

flesh more than just skin and lives you shed
while sleeping.

Snake arms, unknown breasts, damaged
hips and feet a jigsaw puzzle impossible to re-form.

ii. Legs of parchment,
how strong, how fragile.

Twenty-six bones in each foot, thirty joints.
Ligaments, tendons, muscles, nerves,

a complex map on your physio's table. Your body
rewritten by pain, yoga poses you cannot strike,

not this month nor the next. The words you write
in your running journal – *one step at a time*.

If worry is the whetstone, fear the blade,
cast both aside. You are as nature made you,

and nature will heal you or take you
in good time.

ACKNOWLEDGEMENTS

Love and thanks especially to the women in my family – Auntie Lila, Auntie Pat (always missed), Mom, my sister Lee, my niece Phoenix, my daughters-in-law Rachel and Dallas, my sisters-in-law Val, Joni, and Esther, and the memory of my Grans, who led the way with grace, humour, and grit.

Love always to my sons, Darl and Dailyn, for faith and lifelong learning, and to my big brothers, Blaine and Brad, for their stalwart support.

This book is about the strength of women, and women friends. Without you, my life is so much less. Amy Jo Ehman, Rosemary Griebel, Sarah-jane Newman, Gail Norton, Vijay Kachru, Phyllis McCord, Shon Profit, Sharon Osborne, Catharine Hortsing, Kathleen Wall, Tonya Lailey, Noelle Chorney, Jenn Sharp, Jenni Lessard, Madhur Anand. And those whose names are not included here! I love you all. I am blessed.

Thank you to Frontenac House for seeing beauty in Jeanne Dark's vision of women in a dark world. Italian cookies and ongoing gratitude to publisher Neil Petrunia for his faith, and for nosing forward the frontier of poetry. Kudos as well for Neil's layout and design acumen that produced a beautiful book and cover that does honour to its ideas. *Grazie* to Terry Davies for meticulous copy editing and sensitive awards submissions, and Skylar Kay for publicity. Especially, thank you and champagne magnums to senior acquisitions genie and my beloved editor, the marvellous and insightful Micheline Maylor, for feeling the magic, seeing the flaws, and helping me polish the facets. Jeanne Dark's welcome as part of the Frontenac family means more than almost everything (except maybe that first morning cup of good coffee!).

Thank you to Stacey Walyuchow for *The Reckoners,* your breathtaking art that so perfectly portrays the spirit of Jeanne Dark.

Thank you to the Saskatchewan Writers Guild for the many ways the Guild supports the writers of Saskatchewan, particularly the John Hicks Long Manuscript Award, writing group grants, annual writing retreats, and the Virtual Writer in Residence program.

For inspiration, thank you to Sage Hill Writing, its past directors, and its current executive director, singer-poet Tara Dawn Solheim. Much gratitude for generosity and wisdom to Tim Lilburn, Don McKay, and the Sage Ones of the 2013 and 2017 spring poetry colloquia. Thank you especially to Tim Lilburn for permission to use his words as an epigraph for this book. The quoted lines come from *Living in the World As If It Were Home* (Corbel Stone Press, UK, 2016).

Deepest thanks and bottles of Viognier to Maureen Scott Harris and Leslie Vryenhoek, for perceptive readings of earlier drafts.

Coffee, chocolate cakes, and gratitude to Sheri Benning, Susan Musgrave, Sylvia Legris, Sheri-D Wilson, Louise Bernice Halfe Sky Dancer, Sue Goyette, Lorna Crozier, and Jeanette Lynes, for your leadership as poets and mentors. And to the many women poets whose work continues to inspire me, *milles mercis*.

Thank you to my wonderful colleagues in Visible Ink for years of collectively working to improve our work and our wee corner of the world – Lisa Bird-Wilson, Rita Bouvier, Andréa Ledding, Murray Lindsay, Regine Haensel, Gayle Smith.

Thank you to St. Peter's Abbey in Muenster, Saskatchewan, for peace, shelter, sustenance, cookies, collegiality, quinzhees, and peanut-loving chickadees.

Thank you to the generous members of the Saskatchewan and Canadian writing communities.

My appreciation to the publishers and editors of the small presses across the country that continue to publish Canadian writers in literary magazines and books. Thanks in particular to those listed in my publication credits.

Hearts and flowers, supper and bubbles to my husband Dave Margoshes, who is my first reader and best love.

Author photo credit and sincere gratitude to Richard Marjan.

In the spirit of reconciliation, I acknowledge that I live, work, write, and play on the traditional territories of the Cree, Saulteaux, Nakoda, Dakota, Lakoda, and Dene People, the homeland of the Métis Nation, and all people who make their homes in the Treaty 6 region of Central Saskatchewan. I gratefully recognize the bond between us and the living creatures, skies, lands, and waters.

Peace.

PUBLICATION CREDITS

In literary journals:
"Marilyn (un)dressed" appeared as "Marilyn" in *The Quint*, Vol. 2.2, Feb 2010.

"Sharing Mason jars" appeared in *Gastronomica*, Vol. 12, No. 3, Aug 2012.

"Cassandra the seer" appeared in *Canadian Literature*, Fall 2017.

"Sharpen" appeared in *The Antigonish Review*, Spring 2018.

"Jeanne Dark's fear of bridges" appeared as "Fear of bridges" in *The Society*, Spring 2018.

"Amelia, vanished" appeared in *untethered*, Vol. 4.1, Spring 2018.

"Jeanne Dark contemplates the sky" appeared in *The Society*, Spring 2020.

"Lines of lamentation" appeared as "Kaddish" in *Grain*, Vol. 48.4, Summer 2021.

"The Only" appeared as "Suppers at The Only" in *Grain*, Vol. 48.4, Summer 2021.

"Departure" appeared in *FreeFall*, Vol. 33, No. 1, Spring 2023.

"Fledgling" appeared in *The Literary Review of Canada*, Volume 31, Number 2, April 2023.

As chapbooks:
Jeanne Dark comes of age on the prairie (Espresso Chapbooks, edited by Cary Fagan and Rebecca Comay, Summer 2019). Espresso Chapbooks is an editorial collective made up of Fagan, Comay, and Bernard Kelly. Gorgeous chapbooks made by purists, hand-sewn and hand-bound, published in a limited and numbered print run of 100 copies.

"That night at Mountain Mecca" appears in a chapbook anthology, *Works For Now* (Espresso Chapbooks, edited by Cary Fagan and Rebecca Comay, Summer 2020).

In anthologies:
"Consider the bus driver" appears as "A Consideration of the bus driver" in *Resistance: A Poetic Response to Sexual Assault* (University of Regina Press, edited by Sue Goyette, spring 2021).

"Where stones gather" appears as "Hunting" in *Line Dance* (Burton House Books, edited by Gerald Hill, 2016).

"Curatives for morning sickness" was a shortlisted finalist for *Room*'s 2018 poetry contest.

"Suppers at The Only" was a longlisted finalist in *The New Quarterly*'s Nick Blatchford Occasional poem contest in 2012.

NOTES

"Marilyn (un)dressed" (page 27):

This poem was written after viewing "Some Like it Haute: The Costumes of Marilyn Monroe" at the Glenbow Museum, Calgary, Alberta, in 2008.

"Quotidian, female" (page 31):

[1] Prosecutor Michael Petrie read the families' impact statements when Robert Pickton was convicted of the murders of six women on December 11, 2007.

[2] From the statement of Elaine Belanger, mother of Brenda Wolfe, as read by Prosecutor Petrie.

[3] Soraya Bahgat, a women's rights advocate and co-founder of Tahrir Bodyguard, a group that rescues women from assault.

"Jeanne Dark comes of age on the prairie" (page 42):

This long intertextual poem originated in April 2016, when Saskatchewan's then-Poet Laureate Gerald Hill sent out daily two-line prompts to Saskatchewan Writers Guild members from poems by Saskatchewan poets to celebrate National Poetry Month. I saved the lines, and two months later, I wrote the entire work in a blinding four-hour marathon on the banks of the Bow River in Calgary while visiting long-time friends. My gratitude and blessings on the Muse and my friends. The poets (and/or their publishers and/or literary executors) whose lines are included have all granted their permission for their use here. My thanks to Gerry Hill and to the poets whose work lit Jeanne Dark's path.